By Wendy Mass and Michael Brawer

Illustrated by Elise Gravel

LITTLE, BROWN AND COMPANY
New York   Boston

Text copyright © 2014 by Wendy Mass and Michael Brawer
Illustrations copyright © 2014 by Elise Gravel

Little, Brown and Company

Hachette Book Group
237 Park Avenue, New York, NY 10017
Visit our website at lb-kids.com

Little, Brown and Company is a division of Hachette Book Group, Inc.
The Little, Brown name and logo are trademarks of Hachette Book Group, Inc.

The publisher is not responsible for websites (or their content) that are not owned by the publisher.

First Edition: April 2014

Library of Congress Cataloging-in-Publication Data

Mass, Wendy, 1967– author.
    Space taxi / by Wendy Mass and Michael Brawer ; illustrated by Elise Gravel. — First edition.
        pages cm
    Summary: On "Take Your Kid to Work Day," eight-year-old Archie discovers that his father drives a space taxi that shuttles aliens from one area of the universe to another.
    ISBN 978-0-316-24319-3 (hardcover) — ISBN 978-0-316-24320-9 (paperback) — ISBN 978-0-316-24321-6 (electronic book) — ISBN 978-0-316-24333-9 (electronic book—library edition)   [1. Interplanetary voyages—Fiction.   2. Adventure and adventurers—Fiction.   3. Fathers and sons—Fiction.]   I. Brawer, Michael, author.   II. Gravel, Elise, illustrator.   III. Title.
    PZ7.M42355Sp 2014
    [Fic]—dc23

                                                                                              2013021622

HC: 10 9 8 7 6 5 4 3 2
PB: 10 9 8 7 6 5 4 3 2 1

RRD-C

Printed in the United States of America

To our favorite copilots,
Griffin and Chloe

CONTENTS

Chapter One:

Take Your Kid to Work Day.....1

Chapter Two:

Barney's Bagels and Schmear.....8

Chapter Three:

The Next Town Over.....18

Chapter Four:

The Trip.....30

Chapter Five:

The Fare.....45

Chapter Six:

A Ratty Ball of Fur.....60

Chapter Seven:

A New Job.....70

Chapter Eight:

Home, Sweet Home.....87

Three Science Facts to Impress Your
Friends and Teachers.....99

Chapter One:
Take Your Kid to Work Day

Beep! Beep! Beep! Beep!

It's not every day a regular kid like me gets to wake up at midnight. But this is no regular day. Today is Take Your Kid to Work Day, and I'm going to ride with Dad in his taxi! Dad works the night shift, so he's usually awake when I'm asleep and asleep when I'm awake. But not tonight.

I've been waiting eight years, eight months, and eight days for this day to arrive. Instead of staring at the maps of the big city taped to my walls, I'll actually get to go places. Mom likes to keep us close to home, but I'm itching to explore. My little sister, Penny, is the same way. Any open door and she takes off like she's late for something important.

Mom sticks her head in my room. "Archie Morningstar, aren't you up yet? Dad's waiting outside."

Mom always uses my full name when she wants to make sure I'm paying attention. I wish I had a normal last name that no one would tease me about. The *real*

Morning Star is a nickname for the planet Venus, which is so bright you can still see it as the sun rises. Maybe Morningstar would be a cool name if I lived in the country and could actually *see* the stars and planets. But here in the city all we can see is bright lights and smog.

I jump out of bed, fully dressed.

She frowns. "Did you even sleep at all? It's going to be a long night and you don't want to fall asleep on the job."

I shake my head. "I was too excited to sleep. But I'm not tired, I promise." I hurry over to the window. Dad's yellow taxi gleams under the streetlight. He keeps it really clean, even though it's old and clunky and most mornings he comes home without any hubcaps on his tires.

I push up my window. "I'm coming, Dad!"

Mom groans. "Archie, it's midnight. You probably woke your sister. And half the block."

"Oops, sorry." I run over to my desk and grab the one thing I don't go anywhere without—the metal tube my grandpa gave me before he retired to Florida. It looks kind of like an empty paper-towel roll, but it's black with a single silver star painted on it. I bring it with me to baseball practice, to school, even to the bathroom! My friends are so used to seeing it they don't even tease me anymore. Well, not much, anyway. When Grandpa gave it to me, he told me I'd need it one day and I'd know when that day arrived. So until that day comes, it goes where I go. "See ya later, Mom!"

"Archie, wait," she says.

I stop, pretty sure she's going to tell me to leave the tube at home, like she always does.

But Mom doesn't mention the tube. Instead, she hands me a brown bag and a warm thermos. It's the same thing she gives Dad before he leaves every night. It would be dorky to show how cool I think this is, so I just take it and mumble, "Thanks."

"Let me take one last look at you," she says, wiping her eyes. "I never thought this day would come. I'm going to miss you."

Mom can be so mushy, always hugging and smooching me. She doesn't like it when

I complain that I'm too old for that stuff. So I hold in my groan and say, "Oh, Mom. I'm only going to the other side of town."

"Well...it may be a little farther than that, honey." She pulls me in for a hug.

"I'll be fine," I tell her, squirming away after what I feel is a reasonable period of time. "I'll be with Dad."

She opens her mouth to say something, but instead she kisses me on the cheek, whispers, "I love you, honey," and shuts the door behind me.

CHAPTER TWO:
Barney's Bagels and Schmear

With my supplies in hand, the dark night before me, and Mom inside, I'm feeling pretty grown up right about now. I hold up my thermos and paper bag. "Hi, Dad, I'm ready to go to work!"

He lets out a deep, rumbly laugh.

"Buckle up then, Archie! You're in for a wild ride."

I carefully place Grandpa's tube on the floor behind my seat and put my seat belt on. The old taxi rattles and groans as we pull away from the curb. I don't think the ride's going to get too wild. Our biggest adventure will probably be going over a bump and losing a hubcap!

I've never heard the streets so quiet. It's almost spooky. I shiver, even though it's not cold. I have to remember not to let my imagination run away with me. That's what Mom used to tell me when I was a little kid and thought a four-armed, three-eyed alien was living under the kitchen sink. Plus, I'll be with Dad, and he does this every night.

I look around at the empty streets. "How do you find someone who needs a ride?" I ask.

"I get my assignments from the depot," Dad explains. "Then I go pick up my fare. That's what we call the person—or people—who need a ride. Then I take them wherever they want to go. It's different every night. And tonight I'll have my best pal along for the ride. Sounds like an adventure, right?"

Feeling better, I smile back at him. "Right, Dad!"

A few minutes later we pull up in front of Barney's Bagels and Schmear. It's not closed for the night like the rest of the restaurants and stores in the area. Through the large window I can see that half the tables are full with people eating, sipping coffee, talking, and laughing.

"Our first stop," Dad says, turning off the car.

"But Mom already gave us food," I say, pointing to the brown bag at my feet.

"That's breakfast," he says with a grin. "This is a midnight snack."

As Dad pushes the door open, all the eyes in the place look up. Some people shout, "Hey, Morningstar, how's it going?" Others wave or give the thumbs-up sign. Dad shouts back greetings and leads me to the counter. For a second I think I see what looks like a dog wearing headphones slip out the back door. I rub my eyes. Mom was right. I probably should have gotten some sleep.

Dad orders us each a tuna sandwich on a bagel, along with a coffee for him and an apple juice for me.

"Is this your boy?" the man asks as he neatly slices our poppy-seed bagels. He has a big, round belly and a happy smile.

Dad nods and pats me on the shoulder. "This is Archie. He's eight years, eight months, and eight days old today."

"Big day for you, eh, young Morningstar?" the man says, and then winks. At least I think he winked. Maybe a poppy seed flew into his eye.

I almost tell him that it's a big *night* for me, not day, but Mom always says it's rude to correct people. So I just nod and say, "I've never seen the city at night before."

"You're gonna see a lot more than that," he says, winking again. Those poppy seeds must really fly! Someone behind us chuckles and I turn around. For a split second it looks like a lady sitting at the counter has one more head than she's supposed to have. But when I blink again, she goes back to normal.

Okay, I *definitely* see a nap happening in my near future.

On the way out of the deli, Dad stops at almost every table. How does he know all these people? When we get to the street, I ask, "Are we going to the depot now?"

"We just did," he replies, pulling a slip of paper from the bag holding the sandwiches.

"Huh?" I look behind us at the bagel shop. All the customers are crowded by the window, watching us. When they see me looking, they quickly run back to their seats. Life after midnight is weird.

"Let's go, son." Dad steers me toward

the car. He hands me the piece of paper and says, "Our first pickup awaits."

I read the handwritten words:

Mr. Ramsey Fitch
751 Zoder Street,
Apartment C
Delta Three, South Quadrant,
Cygnus Galaxy

Not to brag, but I'm pretty familiar with the city. I've memorized all the maps on my walls. I've never seen any South Quadrant, Cygnus Galaxy. When we're both in the car, I ask, "Is this on the other side of the city, Dad?"

He smiles. "It may be a little farther."

My eyes widen. "You mean like the next town over?"

He smiles again and pats my knee. "Something like that."

I buckle up in a hurry. Forget the nap—I'm way too excited now. A midnight visit to the next town over. Wait till the kids at school hear about this!

Chapter Three:
The Next Town Over

The car starts with its usual clanging and banging. Once we're on the road, I ask, "Hey, Dad, how do you know all those people in the bagel place?"

"Oh, I've known them for years," he says, adjusting his rearview mirror. "Most of them are drivers, like me. Some are copilots."

"Copilots? Taxi drivers have copilots?"

He laughs. "Of course. We'd get hopelessly lost without them."

"But *you* don't have one."

"I used to. Yesterday was his last day."

"Huh? But you never—" Suddenly the dashboard lights up in a rainbow of colors. Buttons, knobs, and screens pop out of the flat surface. My eyes bug out of my head. That definitely did *not* happen on the way to the restaurant!

Dad reaches for a knob marked COM LINE and twists it two notches to the left. "Sal Morningstar reporting for duty."

"Good evening, Morningstar," a squeaky voice crackles through the car. "This is

Home Base. Do you have the instructions for your first pickup?"

"Affirmative. I'm heading to the field now."

Field? What field? The only field I know of in the city is the one I play Little League baseball on, and we already passed it.

"Be careful out there," the voice warns. It sounds like a mouse in a cartoon.

"Always am," Dad replies. "Morningstar out." He turns the knob back again without even looking.

"What was *that* about, Dad? What's a com line?"

"That's how I communicate with Home Base," he replies, veering the car hard to the left.

"What's Home Base?" I twist around in

my seat and look behind us. Where did the city go? It's so dark. "Where are we?"

"Hold on, Archie!" We whiz past a sign that says AIRFIELD.

"Um, Dad?" I grip the sides of my seat with all my strength. "Aren't airfields where planes take off?"

"Yup!" Dad says. Before I can even form my next thought, a second seat belt reaches across my body and pins me tightly to the back of the seat.

The car grunts, and even in the darkness I can tell it's changing. The hood stretches out until it's much longer and rounder. The roof grows higher above our heads. "Dad! Are those... *WINGS*?" I have to shout over the sound of the engine, which is getting louder with every second.

A keypad swooshes out from the dashboard, and Dad's right hand flies over the keys.

"Dad!" I shout. "Can you please tell me what's going on? I thought you were a taxi driver!"

"I am, son. Now, this is gonna feel a bit strange, but trust me, you're totally safe."

I tighten my grip on the arms of my seat. Dad presses a red button and... *BANG! BOOM! KA-BLAMO!*

Fire explodes from the back of the car. We zoom down a runway that I didn't even see in the dark. All four hubcaps fly off and spin in different directions. We're going so fast I don't even hear them land. And then, before I can catch my breath, we're going UP! Straight UP! Into the SKY!

I want to ask Dad if I'm dreaming, but

I can't seem to make words come out of my mouth. My heart is thumping so loudly I bet Mom can hear it back home.

Mom!

She would FREAK OUT if she knew about this! If I ever make it home again, she can hug me as long as she wants. Seriously. And I won't complain about the kisses, either. I'll even take 'em from Penny, and hers usually leave a smear of peanut butter on my cheek.

My jaw drops as we pass the moon.

THE MOON!

I've never been on an airplane before, but I'm pretty sure we're not supposed to be this high.

Dad's talking and pointing out the window, but I can't focus on a word he says. He pulls a lever below the steering wheel and we slow down a little. I finally remember to breathe. We are still moving really, REALLY fast, though.

I begin to notice the stars. Lots and lots of stars. More stars than I ever imagined existed. I stare and stare. I can't see the moon anymore. Is that...*Saturn*? We swerve to the right to avoid what looks like a giant chunk of ice, then bank to the left.

It's a good thing we haven't eaten those tuna sandwiches yet. Mine would be splattered all over the windshield by now.

"Here, Archie," Dad says, handing me a rolled-up paper scroll.

I stare at him. He *looks* like my dad. He *sounds* like my dad. But we're in OUTER SPACE and he doesn't seem NEARLY as surprised as he should be.

"It's a map," he explains, pointing to the

scroll clutched in my hand. "I'll need you to tell me when we reach the third wormhole. They're invisible, of course."

I want to shout, "THERE ARE GIANT WORMS MAKING HOLES IN OUTER SPACE AND YOU WANT ME TO *FIND* ONE? On *PURPOSE*?" But I'm still too shocked to speak. I unroll the paper and spread it out on my lap. This is not easy because my hands won't stop shaking.

The map isn't like any I've ever seen. Thick green lines crisscross each other, dotted here and there with red and blue splotches, and in the center is one small yellow circle. Tiny numbers are printed along each line in some sort of pattern. "Um, Dad? I have no idea what I'm looking at." My voice comes out weird, like a croaking frog. A really freaked-out croaking frog.

25

"You can do this, son. Just give it a try."

"But I don't—"

He pats my knee. "You'll figure it out. I *should* mention, though, if we miss the wormhole, I'll be late for my pickup. And late getting you back home. And then we'll both have to deal with your mother."

I stare at him, then back at the map. This is crazy. Why would Dad think I could see something that's invisible? I stare hard at the paper, but all I see are those lines and numbers and dots.

And then...*BAM!* Right in front of my eyes it changes. The images on the map rise off the paper and I'm staring at a 3-D image of outer space. It's hovering right there over my lap! The small yellow circle is now a perfect image of our taxi! Is

that...yes! I can see me and Dad inside, zooming through space.

The images of the planets and stars are so real I almost feel like I can reach out and touch them. So I do! As soon as my finger lands on one of the glowing spheres, the air around the object fills with information. I touch a wormhole (which, invisible or not, I can clearly see), and words pop up to tell me that a wormhole is a tunnel connecting two distant points in space.

I look at Dad in amazement. "How does this...what...why...?" I can't seem to make the words come out right.

Dad laughs. "You see it now, don't you?"

"I see...everything! The whole universe, I think."

"It must be quite amazing."

"Can't you see it, too?" I ask, surprised.

He shakes his head.

"Why not?" I ask.

"I'll explain later," he says, speeding up again. "Right now I need you to guide me to the third wormhole. Make sure it's the third, and not the fourth."

My heart thumps loudly again as I try to sort out the different wormholes. They all look the same. "What happens if I choose the fourth by mistake?"

Dad shudders. "Let's hope we never find out."

Chapter Four:
The Trip

"Turn right!" I shout. "Now, Dad!"

Dad yanks the wheel and shouts, "Yee-ha!"

We plunge into the wormhole, and the night takes on a whole new level of strange. The stars disappear like someone turned off a huge switch in the sky. Streaks of color fly past our windows almost faster than I can see them. I gasp as we twist and turn like we're on the universe's longest roller coaster. I think I'm going to be sick.

On the plus side, no real worms.

The whole time we're on this crazy ride, Dad is leaning back in his seat, grinning wildly. He looks like a kid who just found out he's going to Disney World instead of the dentist's office.

"I knew you could do it, Archie!" Dad says, beaming at me. "The day you were born, your grandpa bet you'd be an even greater space map reader than him. And he was one of the best!"

I try to answer, but the car plunges into

a series of loop-de-loops. I clamp my lips and eyes shut.

"It'll straighten out in a few seconds," Dad promises as the car flips upside down for the third time.

They are a few LONG seconds, but finally we stop looping and enter an area of gentle curves. I open my eyes and take a few deep breaths before saying, "Grandpa was a *space map reader*? But he sold hats for a living."

Dad shakes his head. "And he didn't retire to Florida, either. He's currently tanning himself on a planet where one of three suns is always shining."

"There's a planet with three suns?"

Dad spreads his arms wide. "You wouldn't BELIEVE the kinds of planets there are. The universe is an amazing place, Archie. I'm so glad you're finally getting to see it."

The map on my lap flattens with a faint *whomp*. All the spinning planets and fiery stars have become simple lines and dots again.

"Um, Dad?" I ask. "Are you sure I'm not dreaming all this?"

He shakes his head. "Nope. All real."

"But...all these years, why did you tell me you drove a taxi?"

"I *do* drive a taxi," he says. "It just happens to be a *space* taxi." He leans over and pats the dashboard. "Top of the line, I might add. It only clunks and groans to blend in with regular taxis on Earth."

I stare at him as he keeps talking.

"Our family has been in the space taxi business for five generations," he says. "I'm a driver. I can take my fares anywhere in the universe and still get home in time for breakfast." He clasps me on the shoulder. "And you're a copilot, Archie! Being able to read a space map is a very special talent that runs in families. My father had it, so I'd hoped you'd get it, but I didn't know for sure until today—when you turned eight years, eight months, and eight days old!"

I shake my head. It all sounds too crazy. "But, Dad, what if choosing this wormhole was just a lucky guess? Maybe we're really in the fourth one, or the second."

He shakes his head. "Trust me, we'd know by now. You're a copilot, all right."

I narrow my eyes at him. "Does Mom know about this?"

Dad laughs. "Of course. You know how hard it is to hide things from your mother."

It's true. Mom can tell if one jelly bean is missing out of a whole bowl. And she always knows *I'm* the one who took it.

"Look," Dad says, pointing ahead of us. I can see two tiny dots of light far in the distance. As we get closer, they grow bigger and bigger. The dashboard springs to life again in a flash of color and sound. Dad takes hold of the wheel.

"We'll need the map," he says. "We're nearing the orbit of Delta Three."

"There's a planet out there?" I ask, seeing nothing planetlike at all.

"Yup. And we're approaching its two suns." Dad hands me a pair of sunglasses and I put them on just in time. We fly out of the wormhole and zip between two *huge* balls of bright yellowish-red flame. For a few seconds the air in the taxi grows superhot, before returning to normal.

At that moment the high-pitched, squeaky voice crackles through the car again. I jump in my seat, surprised anything could still startle me.

"Morningstar, this is Home Base. Please report your current location."

Dad turns the com line knob on. "We're on approach to our pickup on Delta Three."

"Phew!" The voice sighs. "You made it into the right wormhole!"

"Sure did. Thanks to my son, the copilot!"

"Congratulations, young Morningstar," the voice says.

I smile weakly, still not totally convinced

it wasn't beginner's luck. The map in my lap pops up again. I focus in on the tiny image of the yellow taxi hovering above my knee. It's heading right toward a blue-green planet the size of a marble. I look out the windshield. Right in front of us is also a blue-green planet, but it's MUCH bigger than a marble. This must be Delta Three. If it weren't for the two suns, I'd think we were looking down at Earth. This is what the globe in my classroom looks like.

"What do I do, Dad?"

"I'll need you to tell me when we're about to enter the upper atmosphere. It should be around fifteen miles from the planet. Then I'll reverse the thrusters to slow us down. Sound good?"

"Um, sure," I say, not sure at all. I know

from school that the atmosphere surrounds a planet and protects it from the sun and maybe other stuff, but that doesn't mean I know what it looks like.

"And, Archie, I probably don't need to tell you this, but if I don't slow us down in time, well..." He trails off, but I get his message loud and clear.

I gulp and touch the image of the little yellow taxi floating above the map. Lines instantly shoot out of it, with numbers running above them. I quickly realize the numbers are showing me how far we are from the objects around us. The closest is Delta Three, at only forty miles. I breathe a sigh of relief. Archie Morningstar, World's Best Space Taxi Copilot, has done it again. "Reverse thrusters on the count of three... two...one...now!" I shout.

The number on the map changes to fifteen miles. Dad grabs a red handle above his head and pulls it all the way down. The engine grinds and whirs and the taxi shakes, but we don't seem to be losing any speed. The planet is getting closer and bigger by the second. I push my back into the seat, and my hands clamp down on the armrests. Did I mess up? Maybe the numbers mean something else? Maybe they mean how many feet away we are, not miles?

Just when the planet seems close enough to reach out and touch, the front of the taxi tilts up, and we finally slow down. Instead of flying headfirst toward the ground, we're now flying parallel to it, so that's a lot less scary. A loud rumbling sound fills the car.

"Landing gear," Dad explains before I can ask.

We weave past buildings (all painted pink for some reason) and houses (also pink) and trees (still green) until we circle above a landing field that looks just like the one on Earth. For a split second I wonder if Dad's been playing some crazy trick on me and we're actually back home. "Morning-star and son, coming in for a landing," Dad says, and sets us down so gently I don't realize we're on the ground until he says it.

We roll to a stop at the end of a run-way. The car shudders back to its original taxi-like state, and Dad drives us out to the road. I had expected aliens to have green skin and tentacles, or maybe scales and five legs. But the people we pass on the street look human, only everyone is really tall, with short hair and long arms and legs, and they kind of glide when they walk.

They must have some really good bas-ketball games here.

A few minutes later we pull up in front of an ordinary-looking apartment building, not much different from our own. Besides the pinkness, I mean.

Dad turns off the car, which gives one last sputter and clunk before going quiet. "We're here!" he says with a grin. "Your first visit to another planet!" As though he's reading my mind, he says, "I know it looks a lot like home. Planets need to follow the same sort of rules in order for life to exist. Wait till you see the Gamma Quadrant, though. Man, the planets in those galaxies are downright weird!"

I grin. "Does that mean you'll take me to work again someday?"

He laughs and undoes his straps. "Let's

get through today first, and then we'll see. Ready?"

I nod. I'm about to step onto another planet! I take a deep breath, step out of the car, and instantly begin rising up into the air.

I repeat, I AM FLOATING IN THE AIR. Like a BALLOON! Soon I'm almost as high as the trees lining the street. I should be freaking out, but once you've loop-de-looped through a wormhole and almost plunged headfirst into a planet, this doesn't seem so scary.

Still, a little warning might have been nice.

Chapter Five:
The Fare

AH-CHOO!

Dad freaks out enough for both of us. "Archie!" he yells, running around underneath me. "Grab on to a branch! Quick, before you get higher than the trees!"

I reach out with both arms and legs until I'm able to grab the top branch of the closest tree. The trees on this planet are very tall, much taller than on Earth. I wrap myself around the trunk and hold tight. The suns are pretty bright up here, but luckily I still have my sunglasses on.

"Great job, Archie!" Dad calls, running over to my tree. "Can you climb down?"

I nod. The bark is kind of rough, but when I loosen my grip, I can feel myself start to float again. So I hang on tight and begin climbing down. Around halfway to the ground I'm feeling pretty good about my climbing abilities. A city kid like me doesn't get many chances to climb trees. I should go to the park more often.

"That's it, Archie," Dad calls up. "Keep going."

Still gripping tight with my hands

and feet, I lower myself one more branch. *Whoa!* I suck in my breath. Six inches away from my face is a large white ball of fur. The ball of fur's belly is rising and falling with each breath. I don't dare move. Who knows what a space animal could do to a kid? Drag me back to its cave? Swallow me in one gulp?

The branch creaks. I wince as the creature lifts his head and looks right at me. He has long whiskers, triangle-shaped ears, and bright green eyes.

"Meow," he says, lazily cleaning a paw with his tongue. As he rolls to the side, I can see a few gray patches of fur on his belly. I had been afraid of a cat! A cat that pretty much looks exactly like a cat from Earth. Bigger and fluffier, but not a scary

eat-my-brains-for-breakfast kind of alien by any means.

I inch closer. The cat swishes his tail but doesn't back away. His tail has an odd green circle around the tip, like someone drew a ring around it with a green marker. He isn't wearing a collar, so I can't tell if he belongs to anyone. Holding on tight to the tree with one hand, I reach out the other so he can sniff it. He must not think I'm much of a threat because he lowers his head and lets me pet him. "How'd you get stuck in this tree?" I murmur as I scratch under his neck. He just purrs happily. Cats have always liked me. I should ask for one as a pet.

"How's it coming, Archie?" Dad calls up between the branches.

I say a fast good-bye to the cat and keep scrambling down the tree.

Once I get low enough, Dad grabs me and lowers me to the ground. I'm *finally* standing on another planet! Pushing down gently, but firmly, on the top of my head to keep me from lifting off again, Dad stuffs what look like yellow marbles into each of my pockets. I can feel them tugging me toward the ground.

"Sorry, son," he says, lifting his hand from my head. "I forgot to give you these gravity balls before we left the car. On Earth each of those would weigh a hundred pounds. You'll need them to stay on the ground. There is slightly less gravity here."

"I think I just found that out."

He laughs. "Indeed you did! Now let's

go pick up Mr. Fitch. We're a little behind schedule."

I'm sure it's my fault that Dad's late. What if his fare is really mad? What if my trouble figuring out the map gets Dad fired?

But when we ring the bell, a man with tan skin and very white teeth opens the door with a smile and a cheerful *"Good day!"* I wonder if this is Mr. Fitch. He doesn't look like the other people we've passed. This guy is large. Like, superlarge. Like, pro-wrestler large. The business suit he's wearing looks like it's about to split wide open.

"Are you ready, sir?" my dad asks.

Mr. Fitch nods and steps out onto the porch beside us. He's carrying a long coat in one hand and a brown briefcase in the other. Except for his size, he could be any regular businessman from Earth. He whistles as he follows us out to the taxi.

"Mr. Fitch?" I ask. "There's a cat stuck up a tree. Is he yours?"

Mr. Fitch stops walking. His smile vanishes. "A cat?" he asks. "I'm allergic to cats. You saw one?"

I nod and point up at the tree. "On that branch. He was white, mostly."

Mr. Fitch reaches up and pushes aside the leaves, but the branch is empty.

"We'd better go, sir," Dad says. "I don't want you to be late for your meeting."

Mr. Fitch takes one more peek into the tree, then shrugs. His smile reappears. "If it was there, it's gone now."

Mr. Fitch is so wide he fills up nearly

all of the backseat. Dad calls Home Base on the com line and tells them we're on our way to the drop-off.

Zooming into outer space is easier once you've done it already. Dad explains that Mr. Fitch's business meeting is on Delta Nine, which is in this same solar system, so we won't need the wormhole. He leans over and presses a small blue button in front of me. A keypad springs out of the dashboard. "All you have to do this time, Archie, is map out the most direct route, then program it in with the keypad."

"No problem," I tell him, trying to sound confident so Mr. Fitch won't know I've never done this before. I lean over the map and whisper, "Map, show me Delta Nine." And just like that, the map springs to life. I can see not only Delta Nine but the whole route between it and us. I hadn't really expected that to work!

Apparently, we will have to avoid two solar storms, three asteroid belts, and what looks like a bus full of tourists, but other than that, it's a straight shot. I use the keypad to type in the quickest and safest route. I'm amazed that I can do what I'm doing. I bet I totally ace my next math test.

"Can't we go any faster?" Mr. Fitch asks. His smile is fully gone now. He sneezes three times in a row, blows his nose loudly, then he sneezes some more.

Uh-oh, I must be the reason he's sneezing! I slowly slide down in my seat. Hopefully he won't notice I have a few stray cat hairs on me. I look down at my pants. Okay, more than a few. I pull off one particularly puffy ball of fur and toss it to the floor. That cat sure sheds a lot!

Dad pulls a box of tissues from a hidden storage compartment between our seats. He closes the lid before I can see what else is in there. This car has so many secrets! I hope I get to see more of them soon.

Mr. Fitch scowls and grabs the tissues. The sneezing lasts the entire way to Delta Nine.

This planet is very far away from the two suns that were so bright on Delta Three. The dim reddish light makes the planet look kind of gloomy. The leaves on the thin trees are a gray silver, and the roads have deep cracks in them. Dad quickly drives us to a downtown area and pulls up to the curb in front of a row of gray, lopsided buildings. The people walking on the street wear gray clothes and gray hats, and have gray-colored skin. They don't look unhappy, though. I guess they don't know that their planet is kind of, well, *gray*. I won't need my sunglasses here.

"You'll want to leave your gravity balls in the car," Dad tells me. "Otherwise you'd step out and sink deep into the ground."

At least this time he warned me.

With one last sneeze, Mr. Fitch grabs his briefcase and pushes open his door. "I will be back in ten minutes," he barks at us. "You will wait here."

Mr. Fitch sure is bossy! He hurries out of the car and ducks into an alley between two buildings.

Dad picks up the bags from Barney's Bagels and Schmear. "Time to eat!" We sit on the curb and dig into our sandwiches. We get some curious looks, and an occasional tip of a hat in our direction, but the people on the street mostly ignore us as they pass.

A glob of tuna falls out of my sandwich and onto the street. A second later a large cat appears out of nowhere and pounces on it. He scarfs it down in one bite. This cat is also white, like the one in the tree on the first planet. "You really do attract cats wherever you go!" Dad says, laughing.

Before I can pet this one, he must smell something he likes even better than the tuna, because he takes off in the same direction as Mr. Fitch. I swear I see a blur of green around his tail as he turns the corner. Must be a space cat thing.

Dad takes a swig from his coffee cup. "I have to check in with Home Base, Archie. Feel free to take a look around. Just make sure I can still see you, okay?"

"Got it," I say, gobbling down my pickle. Space travel makes a guy hungry. A shiny, round object lying on the street near the alley where Mr. Fitch went catches my eye. A large coin maybe? No one else has passed by that way. I wonder if he dropped it.

I turn around to ask Dad what we should do, but he's already in the taxi talking on the com line. He did say I could explore a little. With one last glance at the car, I step away from the curb and head toward the alley.

The silver object turns out to be bigger than I thought, and heavier. I turn it over in my hand. It looks like a giant locket with the letters *ISF* etched onto one smooth side. A groove runs around the edge, but I can't pry it open. Whatever it is, I bet Mr. Fitch would want it back.

I peer into the alley but can't see very far. It's dark and even gloomier than out on the streets. A loud shuffling and crashing comes from the other end of the alley. Maybe that cat knocked over a garbage can?

"Unhand me, you fool!" a man shouts. "You have no idea who you're dealing with!"

I know that bossy voice! Mr. Fitch is in trouble!

Chapter Six:
A Ratty Ball of Fur

"Let me go, I say!" Mr. Fitch shouts. "Help me, someone, help!"

It sounds like he's being robbed! Maybe someone wants his briefcase! I have to help him. Especially after I made him sneeze by petting that cat near his house. Just as I think it, Mr. Fitch starts sneezing again.

I don't want to go down there, but I have to do something. Before I change my mind, I hurl the silver disk thingy as hard as I can. All my Little League training has given me a pretty good arm, and it goes deep into the darkness. I hold my breath, wondering if I just made a huge mistake. Then I hear the object clatter to the ground and break open. The alley is immediately filled with light.

"So that's where that went," an unfamiliar voice says. I look around the alley, but the only person there besides me is Mr. Fitch. He's standing next to a pile of old boxes, blinking in the sudden light and clutching his briefcase.

"You!" he shouts, spotting me. "Space taxi kid!" He pauses to sneeze. "Get this thing off of me!"

I back up a step. "Um...what thing?"

He spins around and flails at something on his back.

My eyes open wide when I see what's actually *on* him. It's the CAT! The white cat is hanging on to the back of Mr. Fitch's suit with his claws! His tail is swishing back and forth, and I can clearly see the green circle around it. The cat sticks his head over Mr. Fitch's shoulder to look at me.

"Young sir," he says in a calm, well-mannered voice. "Thank you for returning my Light Orb. I am an officer of the ISF— that's the Intergalactic Security Force— and this man is my prisoner."

Just when I didn't think my day could get any weirder, along comes a talking cat!

I wonder if cats on Earth can talk, too, but they just hide it.

The cat continues. "If Mr. Fitch comes peacefully, he will save himself a lot of trouble."

"Not going to happen, cat!" Mr. Fitch says. Then he reaches one arm over his head and grabs the cat by the scruff of his neck.

"Look, kid," Mr. Fitch says in a calmer voice. "Who you gonna believe—me, an upstanding citizen of Delta Three, or this ratty ball of fur who must have scored a free ride in your dad's taxi to get here?"

He dangles the cat in front of him.

I step closer to get a better look. It really IS the same cat! So it wasn't my petting him that made Mr. Fitch sneeze the whole ride. It was because the cat was actually hiding IN the car with us!

"Unhand me, you brute!" the cat hollers, waving his paws in the air, claws extended. "You are under arrest for trying to sell secret documents to B.U.R.P., one of the universe's biggest criminal organizations."

"I am merely here on business," Mr. Fitch says. "Then this creature jumped on me. Now be a good boy and go tell your father I am ready to leave. And this little stowaway will be staying behind this time!"

The cat hisses.

I look from one to the other. How am I supposed to know who to believe? Mr. Fitch may be bossy, but that doesn't mean he's a criminal. And he's a grown-up, while the cat, well, he's a *cat*!

Mr. Fitch sneezes. He tightens his grip on the cat, who whimpers.

"What's it gonna be, kid?" Mr. Fitch asks in a low voice.

The cat whimpers again.

Mr. Fitch snarls.

I may not know what's really going on, but I know you shouldn't hold a cat like that. "Quick!" I tell the cat. "He's allergic to you! Ruffle your fur or something."

The cat flails his arms and legs and shimmies his body until dander and fur fly in all directions. Mr. Fitch tries to hold his breath. His face gets redder and redder until he finally has to take a breath. Then he has a massive, snot-filled sneezing fit and loosens his grip, and the cat squirms away.

"This animal doesn't know what he's talking about," Mr. Fitch says, backing away from the cat and holding up his briefcase like a shield. Peering over the top and breathing hard, he says, "There's nothing in here but boring business stuff."

Before my eyes, the cat's tail hinges open right at the green line. A laser light shoots out and zaps a hole in the briefcase! Okay, cats on Earth DEFINITELY can't do that.

Mr. Fitch yelps and drops his briefcase. It crashes to the ground and springs open. Documents marked TOP SECRET: PROPERTY OF THE ISF spill out all over the ground.

"He planted those there!" Mr. Fitch yells, stomping on them. "That cat is setting me up!"

The cat stands up on his hind legs,

unzips a pocket hidden behind a patch of gray fur, and pulls out an official badge. He holds it up so I can see his picture with the words INTERGALACTIC SECURITY FORCE OFFICER printed below it.

Mr. Fitch tries to kick at the badge. The cat twists out of the way before the heavy foot can connect with his paw. Mr. Fitch winds up losing his balance and crashes to the alley floor.

The cat points a paw straight at Mr. Fitch, and a silver rope shoots out from between two claws.

"Oomph!" Mr. Fitch says as the rope tightens around his wrists and ankles. Then he has another sneezing fit.

The cat runs over to me, stands on two legs, and shakes my hand.

At that moment my father rounds the corner of the alley. His eyes widen as he takes in the scene. Then he smiles and shakes his head. "You know, Archie, if you wanted to get a cat this badly, you could have just asked."

We all laugh. Well, not Mr. Fitch.

Chapter Seven:
A New Job

"Intergalactic Security Force officer Pilarbing Fangorious Catapolitus at your service," the cat says, bowing to my father. "Sorry about stowing away in your trunk." To me he says, "I am grateful for your aid, young Earth boy. You are very brave. I will see to it that you are well rewarded."

I blush and finish gathering up the papers while the cat—whose name is way too long for me to remember—tells my dad the whole story. Dad agrees to bring the space cat and his captive to ISF headquarters.

The cat leads a red-faced and sneezing Mr. Fitch into the backseat and buckles him in. Then he nudges him with the tip of his pink nose and Mr. Fitch immediately falls into a deep sleep. That's a handy trick! Maybe I could use that on Penny when she wants to play one more game of pretend-Archie-is-a-horsie.

"How are you holding up?" Dad asks me as we strap ourselves in.

"I'm fine. You know, just a regular day. I copilot a space taxi, almost float off a planet, talk to a cat, help catch a criminal. And all before breakfast!"

He laughs. "It's not over yet."

As I smooth out my map, I ask, "Hey, can the cats on Earth talk, too?"

He shakes his head. "Nope. Only the ones from Friskopolus, otherwise known as the Cat Planet. That's where we're headed now."

Dad tells me the coordinates, and I ask the map to show me Friskopolus. Lines shoot out from the image of the little taxi and I quickly plan out the route. I don't want to brag, but I'm getting good at this. I whisper "thank you" to the map, and it almost seems to quiver a bit in response. Then again, I haven't slept in a really long time.

"So, Cat," Dad says once we're on our way, "how did you know Fitch was headed here?"

The cat pauses from cleaning behind his ear with his paw to answer. "I've been tracking him for months. Following him in my own police car would have been much too suspicious. I'd given up hope until you two came along and I saw my chance. I won't forget you and what you've done to help bring peace to the universe."

"We won't forget you, either," I say. "Um, what was your name again?"

"Pilarbing Fangorious Catapolitus," the cat replies.

I glance at Dad. He shrugs.

I turn back to the cat. "That's a big name for a little cat. Or even a big cat, like you. Do you have a nickname?"

The cat shakes his head.

"Okay. How about I call you...Mr. Bubbles!"

The cat frowns, which is something space cats must be able to do.

"Fluffy?"

He narrows his eyes at me.

"Hmm. You probably won't like Snowball, then."

The cat growls.

Dad and I laugh. "Just kidding," I say. "I'll try to come up with a really good name for a space police cat."

I sit back and enjoy watching all the stars glitter around us like billions and billions of fireflies. It might be years before I get to see this view again. Maybe when I grow up, I could get a job with Dad. That would be so awesome.

Mr. Fitch's snoring from the backseat is actually kind of soothing.

I hear a rustling behind me and turn to look. The cat is digging around in his fur pockets. He pulls out a pair of dark sunglasses and slips them on.

"That's it!" I shout. "I'll call you Pockets!"

The cat shrugs. "That is acceptable."

"What else have you got in there?" I ask, peering over the seat.

"Ah, the question should be what *don't* I have in there." He lifts his shades with one paw and winks at me.

I smile and turn back around. I can see from the map that we're about to reach the planet's atmosphere. A few minutes later our wheels touch down on a busy landing field behind Intergalactic Security Force headquarters. Spaceships and space police cars of all different shapes and sizes are landing and taking off.

We are met by two giant cats wearing official ISF badges around their necks. They place a groggy Mr. Fitch onto the back of a little buggy and drive away with him.

Dad and I follow Pockets into the main building. I have to step over large bowls of water and dishes of cat food scattered across the floor. Little robotic mice dart between our legs. The walls are made of yarn. Cats even bigger and fluffier than Pockets are happily eating, licking their paws, chasing fake mice and each other, and scratching the walls. Some are doing this while holding clipboards or talking on the phone.

"Is everyone in the ISF a cat?" I whisper to Pockets.

He shakes his head. "There are headquarters on one planet in each galaxy. We all work together to bring down B.U.R.P. and help keep the universe safe."

"What does B.U.R.P. even stand for?" I ask.

"No one knows," he admits. "It's a big mystery."

We wind up in a large office where a cat who looks like an older, more grizzled version of Pockets is pacing back and forth, a worried look on his face.

"Hello, Father," Pockets says. "I'm back."

The older cat stops pacing and races over to us. He looks Pockets up and down, then jumps on him and flips him over! Dad and I back away. They meow and roll over each other, swatting each other playfully on the nose.

"I was very worried," his father says, stopping to nuzzle Pockets under the chin with his head.

Pockets bats his father away. "I'm fine, Chief. This was my twentieth mission! Didn't you receive my report? I sent it from the space taxi."

"Yes, I got it. You've always been independent, but it's a parent's job to worry about their child."

"Will you still worry about me like that?" I ask Dad. "When I'm all grown up?"

Before my dad can answer, Pockets says, "Well . . . I'm not exactly all grown up."

"You're not?" I ask.

He shakes his head. "I'm only eight years old."

"You're only eight?" Dad and I shout at the same time.

"That's *my* age!" I add. "You sound a lot more grown up than me. And you can do a LOT more things."

"I was always very advanced for my age," Pockets admits. "My father here is the head of the agency, the chief detective on the force. Everyone knew I'd join one day, so I've been training since I was a small kitten. But enough about me." Turning to his father, he says, "You've read my report, Chief. What do you think about my request?"

The chief looks at me and Dad. "Well, I suppose that's up to the humans to decide."

"What are we deciding?" Dad asks.

The chief clears a hair ball from his throat. "It seems my son here thinks you and *your* son would be very helpful in our mission to take down B.U.R.P. before they're able to take over the universe. You'd be honorary Intergalactic Security Force deputies."

My eyes widen. First I discover I'm a space taxi copilot, then I get to help fight intergalactic crime? This has *got* to be the BEST Take Your Kid to Work Day in the history of the universe. I clutch my dad's arm. "That sounds awesome, doesn't it, Dad? Wait till I tell the kids at school!"

Dad hesitates. "Archie, I know it sounds exciting, but we don't know anything about catching criminals."

"We understand that," the chief says. "But Pilarbing Fangorious thinks—"

"We call him Pockets," I interrupt. "Easier to say."

The chief tilts his head at me. "All right, then. *Pockets* thinks, and I agree, that he would blend in easier if he pretended to be merely a child's pet. Adults say things in front of kids that they would not normally say, and that could come in very handy when spying on a suspect. Also, your space taxi is a perfect mode of transportation. It's fast, it can travel to every corner of the universe, and it doesn't need special permission to land. It would be the perfect cover for our secret missions."

"I'd really like to help you," Dad says.

"But if Archie came on my route with me every night, he'd be too tired to go to school. His education is too important."

Before I can think of an argument to counter that, Pockets steps forward. "I can speak three thousand languages," he says. "And what I know about history and math and science and literature could fill a hundred school libraries. I could teach him when we get home each morning—after he sleeps, of course."

"When *we* get home each morning?" my dad repeats.

"My son would have to come live with you," the chief explains. "He's still a kid, after all. Someone would have to watch over him."

I squeal, which is a little dorky, but I

can't help it. My own crime-fighting cat? How awesome would that be? "Can we do it, Dad? You said you don't have a copilot anymore, and don't you need one? Think of all the things I could learn on the job that I'd never be able to learn in school."

Dad sighs. "I did hope you'd be my copilot one day, Archie, but I thought that day would be far from now. I'll agree to a week and we'll see what happens." He shakes his head. "I don't know what your mom's gonna say about this."

"Yay!" I jump up and down. A week is better than nothing. I'm getting a cat PLUS a friend my own age to hang out with, all rolled into one! And I'll be helping to save the universe every night! Pockets holds his paw up to me.

"High five!" we both say at the same time.

"You wouldn't actually be able to tell your schoolmates about this," Pockets says, suddenly serious again. "Our mission has to remain top secret."

After a flash of disappointment I say, "I understand. I promise."

We high-five again and I can't control my grin.

I turn to my dad. "Thanks for agreeing to this! I bet after a few days Mom will get used to having an alien living with us."

"Oh, it wouldn't be the first time," he says.

I pause. "What do you mean?"

"Bubba from Belora Prime lived under

our kitchen sink for a few weeks while his house was being painted."

My eyes widen, then narrow. "Did he have four arms and three eyes?"

Dad nods.

"I *knew* it!"

Chapter Eight:
Home, Sweet Home

CLINK!

Dad gasses up the taxi while Pockets goes back to his house to get his suitcase. A thick layer of dirt and grime and things that look like barnacles cover the car. Now I understand why Dad washes his taxi every day.

When Pockets shows up at the landing field, he doesn't have anything with him. I hope he hasn't changed his mind.

"Aren't you still coming home with us?" I ask.

He nods.

"Then where's all your stuff?"

He pats his chest and belly. "Right here."

I laugh. "Those are some big pockets!"

Pockets grins, then goes over to his father and nuzzles him under the neck. His father nuzzles him back.

"We'll take good care of him," my dad promises. "And I'll make sure he checks in with you daily."

"He's very good at that," the chief says, getting a little teary. He gives his son one final nuzzle, then turns his attention to Dad. "Now, Morningstar, when you're on a mission, Pilarbing Fang—I mean, *Pockets* is in command. During off-hours, *you* are in control. I'll be meeting with my staff tomorrow to figure out how to make the best use of you."

Watching Dad awkwardly shake the chief's paw is kind of funny. I don't think it would be polite to laugh, though, so I turn it into a cough.

When we get into the taxi, the voice coming out of the invisible speakers is screeching like someone who just stepped with bare feet on hot sand. "This is Home Base!" the voice squeaks angrily. "Morningstar, do you hear me? Repeat, do you hear me?"

"She doesn't sound happy, Dad."

"I've been avoiding calling in," Dad admits. "How could I tell them that my fare turned out to be a criminal and was arrested and I had to make an unscheduled stop with him out cold in my backseat?"

"What did you just say?" the voice screeches in an even higher pitch than usual.

"Oops," Dad says. "Guess I left the com line open." He clears his throat. "Hello, Home Base. I'll explain everything when I get back. Morningstar out." He leans over and turns off the knob just as she screeches, "Oh, no you don't, mister!"

Dad winks and asks, "Are you boys strapped in?"

"Yup," I say.

"Indeed I am," Pockets replies.

As we take off, I turn to Dad and ask, "Why does that Home Base lady have such a squeaky voice? She kinda sounds like a mouse."

Dad laughs. "Not *kinda* like a mouse. She IS a mouse!"

At that, Pockets's ears perk up. "A mouse?" he says. "I've never seen a real one!"

"Don't get any ideas back there," Dad warns, but he's smiling. "That mouse is my boss. That means you two will be working together very closely, Pockets. And *that* means no eating each other."

Pockets mutters something that sounds like "I'd like to see *her* try to eat *me*." Then he reaches into one of his pockets, pulls out a full-size pillow (!), and curls up for a nap.

While he sleeps, Dad and I finally eat the breakfasts Mom packed for us. I gobble down three delicious pancakes. Penny only eats things that start with the letter *P*, so we have a lot of pancakes. I'll eat pretty much anything except broccoli, because why would I want to eat something that looks like a tree? We clink thermoses before taking sips. After traveling millions of light-years from home, my hot chocolate is still warm!

I spend the rest of the trip exploring my map. If I turn it in different directions, it shows me all sorts of amazing things. I can't wait to see what pops up on my next trip. I direct us into the right wormhole to get us back. This time I try to keep my eyes open, even on the stomach-churning parts. The bright colors streak by on all sides. One of them—the red streak—moves more slowly than the rest.

A second later it's right next to the taxi. I push my face against the window to get a better look. Then I jump back in surprise.

A tiny red alien in a tiny bubble-shaped spaceship just WAVED at me! I blink and he's gone. I shake my head. "Um, Dad? Did you happen to see a little red alien outside my window?"

He shakes his head. "Nope. But all these lights can play tricks on your eyes."

"I guess you're right," I say, peering into the emptiness around us.

"You did a great job today, Archie," Dad says. "I'm very proud of you." He reaches over and ruffles my hair.

Normally that would embarrass me, but now it just makes me feel good. "Thank you for trusting me to be your copilot, Dad."

He grins. "When I promised you tonight would be an adventure, I had no idea how right I would be."

I grin back. "Yeah, Dad, you left out a lot of stuff about tonight."

He laughs, then gets serious. "I wanted to tell you everything, Archie. But I had to wait until you were old enough to understand. I think you and I make a great team."

I glance into the backseat at the sleeping cat. We're a team of three now.

Once I get us back through Earth's atmosphere, I roll up my map. I wish I had some way to carry it with me. It's not the kind of thing I can just stick in my pocket, like a certain cat I know. I need a way to keep it safe.

As we get closer to Earth, I see a single bright star hanging alone in the sky, glittering like a diamond. Suddenly I know *exactly* what I need. I reach behind me and feel around on the floor until I find my tube from Grandpa. I pop open the top and slide the map inside. A perfect fit!

"I was waiting for you to figure that out," Dad says, smiling. Then he points east at a ball of light. "Do you know what that is?"

"It's Venus, right? The Morning Star?"

"Indeed it is." Dad aims the taxi so I have the perfect view out the front window. The air around Venus glows with the light of the rising sun. Maybe my last

name isn't so bad. After all, it's the name of a long line of space taxi drivers. And also copilots. And now honorary Intergalactic Security Force deputies saving the universe from the evil B.U.R.P., which, when you think about it, is a much worse name than mine.

Behind me, Pockets yawns and stretches. "Anyone got some tuna?"

Three Science Facts to Impress Your Friends and Teachers

1. Gravity is the invisible force that attracts two objects. The heavier the object, the more gravity it has. Gravity is what keeps the planets in orbit around the sun and keeps all the stuff on Earth from floating into space. The planet called Delta Three that Archie visits in this book is smaller than Earth and weighs less, so it has less gravity. The people who live there are taller, the trees are taller, and it's easier for birds to fly and people to walk.

2. A WORMHOLE is like a tunnel from one part of outer space to another. Picture an apple—it would take a worm less time to go through a hole in the apple than to go around the skin of the apple. Some scientists believe this kind of a shortcut through space might one day be possible.

3. Even though we don't think of it this way, our sun is actually a star. It's just a lot closer to us than any other star. A planet that orbits a star *other* than our own sun is called an EXOPLANET. In order for life as we know it to exist, a planet must not be too close to or too far away from its source of heat (its sun) so that its temperature stays within a certain zone. It needs to have water, oxygen, an atmosphere around it, and the right kinds of chemicals in the ground and air. But that's only life as we know it here on Earth. Other planets could have people or creatures living there that have adapted to their environment as we have adapted to ours. With the help of huge telescopes, astronomers are discovering new exoplanets every day. Someday soon we will surely discover that we are not alone in the vast universe.